O9-BTM-823

IN A FREE COUNTRY

In a free country I would be shot for my thoughts of you.
Where thought was free as radio waves
my mind would broadcast your outrageous beauty.
Naked phantoms of our wild nights
would take every mind by storm.
In your name the slaves of industry and commerce
would revolt, cops would strike,
truck drivers walk off whistling from their loads.
All creatures of the earth would drop their pants
in tribute, they would fornicate pell-mell,
every man, queen, woman, dyke and child.
The old would have the young, every mother her son.
And I would be hunted down, my brain quarantined
in a free country, thinking these last thoughts of you.

HOW TO SURVIVE HEAVEN

I was touching her where she'd never been touched.
The devil was in me. I said:
"If there is no more to heaven than this
I am as good as a dead man."
And she said: "What did you have in mind?"

So I opened one door on a white blizzard of stars
and one to an avalanche of green that was our spring.
When I opened a third we lost our solitude
to a grey parade of souls come down on a rainbow.
"You think big," she said, "beyond immortality and bliss."

Then this lady, with a wisdom beyond her years,
(I'm sure that she has been to heaven before
and knows the ins and outs)
gave me fair warning:
"Lie to the angels about your dreams

or they will confiscate them at the gates
and banish them to the bedrooms of the world.
If there are ghosts around us love,
they are dead men's dreams
no saint could smuggle into paradise."

YOUNG MEN'S GOLD

POEMS BY DANIEL MARK EPSTEIN

YOUNG MEN'S GOLD

THE OVERLOOK PRESS/WOODSTOCK, NEW YORK

Acknowledgement is gratefully made to the following magazines in which these poems first appeared: *The New Republic, The North American Review, The Michigan Quarterly, The Smith, The Paris Review, The Atlantic Monthly,* and *The Virginia Quarterly Review.*

Published in 1978 by
The Overlook Press
Lewis Hollow Road
Woodstock, N.Y. 12498

ISBN: 0-87951-071-4 (cloth)
ISBN: 0-87951-076-5 (paper)
Library of Congress Catalog Card Number: 77-20739

THIS BOOK IS FOR
LINDA STEVENS

ONTENTS

"LA BELLE DAME SANS MERCI"

By the road I saw a sleeping woman
more beautiful than the hovering dream
that battled a nightmare above her head.

And in the forest clearing of her dream
stood a hive of worlds, a honeycomb
where destiny had eaten passageways.
Every cell contained a kingdom and a king
named for his ruling passion and his laws.

I am a cruel judge of nature's kindnesses.
And yet I listened
while each one sang out the ballad of his name,
the voices mellow as a bee's last hoard.
Each king sang in his turn

of Compassion, Grace, Love, Charity and Joy.
          Then Beauty rose
and a hawk dived with a nightmare in his claws.

Let sleeping beauty lie, I thought.
The lashes of her eyes were skirts that fluttered
    as the long horses of her dreams raced under them,
her hair a swirl of midnight at high noon.
And as I brushed the nightmare from her brow

she woke and began to glow
                like a pale bird glutted with fire-flies.
She sat and sang to me
      with such sweetness of calm hatred and revenge
                 I hear her song alone.

THE LATE VISITOR

A lady comes to me at an ungodly hour
and takes off her clothes,
she takes off my clothes. She sits
impossibly calm in the pouring light
of a lamp outside my window.

She reminds me we were immortal,
sloughing our worn skins
every spring, until
one beautiful woman kept her flesh
for fear a lover would not know her.

My lady casts no shadow.
She is clear glass
for inquisitive spirits.
The mirrors in my house
will have nothing to do with her.

NIGHT MEDALLION

My woman is sharper than new truth,
a clean bullethole in thick glass.
Winter cuts its teeth on her, the sun
cuts its hand on her,
she's too hot for the beach, the golden sand
goes all to white crystal under her.

She's so proud, the full moon is her mirror.
When she turns from me I see her face
in the rolling window of heaven
and when she comes barefoot to my bedside,
holding a candle,
an elf skates on my heartstream.
Eager candle, milk my mind of treasons.
She's young and I want to fill her with the world.

AFTER THE WEDDING PARTY

A white-faced mummer bride
and bridegroom antic for the crowd.
They hope the mock veil and stovepipe hat
will decoy what spirits plot
love's ruin: dead fathers, by-gone lovers,
imps of cross-purpose
that twist the sheets and spoil a mother's milk.

And so God speeds the true newlyweds
in immaculate wishes of good will.
Hell's guard is down, they steal away
like the sly heros at the crossroads in old westerns
who get down and walk
while villains chase their riderless horses.

But the lovers have more than clowns and God
to thank for their freedom.
The groom's mother
has taken the devils on herself.
They flutter in her lace bodice
like young crows.

POVERTY

You call to me as if I were in some other bed
or gone gold digging with the sun. In fact
I was dreaming I had ten minutes to haul a fortune
in jewels and coins from the cache of a secret mountain.
An underground river bolted under my boat,
spilled the loot and rushed me back here penniless.
All I could bring home you're holding now
in your hands, the rippling wings of my proud rising.

Tired of small secrets, little gifts,
I conjure this secret mountain between us.
Behold the range of my discretion, even in dreams
when you challenge me from every wind of the compass!
You call to me as from a tall house gratefully burning
while fortunes panic around us, fall like stars.

THE DANCE

Fast clouds, in a big hurry to rain on somebody
but there's blue sky enough for us.
October trees, out of their minds with color,
and you and me like nothing else alive,
cosmic accidents spawned between better judgments.
How can we bring a child into the world?
Everywhere people are starving, loveless, climbing walls,
and here we're hugging and kissing in front of God and everybody
in a park full of cheering trees
and our baby is doing a popular dance in your belly.
There isn't room in our bodies for all this joy!

THE CATCH

Under the dome of hemlocks
a green pool
where the creek breaks
its fall, a boy kneeled
fishing. You were afraid
our baby might spoil
his catch with her singing.
Then you were amazed
at his concentration
on the red bobber
and the sly shadows
that streak like trout,
the fast wishes
a boy mistakes
for the game of his mind.

I'm not superstitious
but I wondered if
the violet butterfly
haunting us in circles
was the soul
of that child's curiosity,
too polite and shy to make
eyes at you openly.
When you lifted your blouse
to feed our daughter
I know he saw that,
the round white gift
he is too old to cry,
too young to sing for.

He reeled his line,
took off for higher ground.
When I looked again
there was a man
his father's age
who smiled at us unabashed.

ON A WINTER MORNING

Running for the bus
I ripped my hand open
on a parking sign.
I was bringing you roses.
They were shivering
in green tissue
in my left hand
when my right caught
the blade of a misdemeanor.
My knuckle bone smiled
like a beaten fighter
then the blood came in bracelets.

I treasured them in the tissue,
swung aboard, paid my fare
and passed into the aisle

of faces shining
on my new hand.
Old men and young girls
stood up for me, offered
their old and new blood,
the family jewels
of America, priding themselves
on my deep color.

Their eyes said take
what you need to see
from us, their arms said
take what you need to walk,
their lips said our bodies
are full of what you wear
on your white sleeve.

WOMAN AT A PROPHET'S GRAVE

He must have been awake the god-long night
before his birth, and brought his own light
with him. I saw it in his blue eyes
struggling open against the day,
in the bud-red hands that reached for my cheeks and hair
in an old friend's recognition. Why,
his first crying was music from an untutored horn,
melodic language I'd no time to learn
before he learned mine. He'd parrot my speech
like an old man and laugh and kick at the cradle-frame.
Mimicry led to question and demand
and at nine months we conversed as children do
in a sandbox, a city dug out at their feet.

My old mother scowled and called for the Bible
as the only suitable primer
for a godless widow and her miracle child.
I was afraid. At twelve months he knew by heart
the wonder tales of the Pentateuch:
creation, the chain of begats, red-handed Cain,
flood and raven, Abraham
with knife upraised above his trusting son.
He laughed with Sarah and the drunken Lot
and chided Moses when he beat the stone.
He recited verse as if each syllable
chiselled the naked tablet of his brain.

He wouldn't sleep, and begged me to read on
through dusk and moonrise when soft moths dove
at the lamp swung above us, singeing their wings.

He laughed and chirped at sunrise like a bird,
as if it were a game, a lark, a gamble
played with nutshells and one capricious pea.
Who knows under what blue night our day will be
when the great magician
shuffles the darknesses and shows his hand?

A secret no mother could keep. I opened
his room to one friend and another
then the neighborhood, the city and the world.
Flashbulbs burned round sunspots on our dreams.
And the magi of the colleges came clucking
with a chorus of throat-clearing and mumbling
their perhapses and points of fact and precedents.
Sceptic eyeballs guarded against truth
as if truth were a dragon with magnetic breath
that froze the needles of delicate instruments,
or an infant fouling his diaper in their hands.
They warned me he was dangerous, a tiger cub
weaned of goat's milk in a mission home,
who kept from meat would rage, maul
the hand that held the bottle to his lips.

I knew my child and smiled at all they said,
yet agreed he might hunger for formula I lacked
in my own breasts and in the cupboard of my heart.

So I let them take him across town
to a school for one student, my marvelous boy,
and they let me come
on Sundays to mark his progress.
With tapes, headsets and a bearded platoon
of eager wizards to catechize my son,
they took to stuffing the plastic duffel of his brain
with numbers, formulae, theorums, God knows what,
the moon's phases, scratch sheets, schedules of the tides,
stock quotes, calendars, air flight patterns.
He became a walking infant weather bureau,
slide rule, thesaurus, oracle and bank,
with stock futures, barometer readings and prophecies,
now fair, now cloudy with a chance of rain.
At four he mastered the Calculus, knew by heart
the fat Greek and Latin Lexicons.
When I visited he leapt into my arms
reproving me from Pindar on time's pace,
Homer on the weather and a brace
of his own sweet verses like butterflies
shaken from hills of goldenrod.
I brought him cakes and mysteries, contraband
jaw breakers and crossword puzzles, anagrams,
hacksaws in the little prisoner's apple pie.

I came home crying and lay my head on my mother's lap
where she sat by the window mending a black dress.
She scolded my tears and cursed
the delinquent angels assigned to attend
the descent of such rare creatures into this world.
She said my boy never had a prayer against the soul
that sneaked into his body's room, the little whirlwind
that fed on drafts
until it blew into a stampede of tornados.
Our blessed children come from a long sleep
in a mountain's spine, a flowerbulb or an apple core;
in their dreams they hear confessions of the new dead.
So when our lovemaking shakes one from the tree
he drops down to us full of gossip and old tales,
parlor tricks and divinations that would amaze
a Pope and put the circuses to shame
if the angel midwives shirked their duty.

One sets his finger on the baby's upper lip
(you see there the valley of forgetfulness)
breaks the circle and silver wisdom of its mouth
like a smoke halo above a prophet's fire.

At five he'd put Plato behind him, Gibbon
and a shelf of world history. He knew
Napoleon's tactics at Arcole and Rivoli,
could summon Thucidides on the Punic Wars.

He rose to meet me, straight back and outstretched hand,
small mouthed smile, a buoyant, regal nod.
With Aristotle my son grew tall,
a furrow made its way along his brow.
At seven he'd exhausted antiquity
and four pale classicists,
discovered three Greek irregular verbs
and a lost tense, the future past-pluperfect,
decoded from line endings of an obscure epic
of Ennius. On to Atomism, Principia Mathematica
and the transformations of Einstein and Lorentz.
At nine my child stopped sleeping
to study the blue light of Hesperus.
He stopped eating when the planet winked at him.

"The head that eye belongs in is my own. See
how she looks beyond light to show my days,
the unborn lives spread out on my coverlet
like a sick child's toys.
Here's a crown, fresh laurel and a mansion,
there's the mob, a dungeon and a blasted tree—"
They sent for me. I held him close and sang
a lullabye that turned to a dirge on my lips
as the child who'd raced from infant to boyhood
skipped manhood for dotage and old age for death.

He lay like a shrunken king in a rustling flock,
the cheated vultures of his unlived days.

Earth and sky, old lovers, come together here
and see how the mother's rewarded for her milk!
I have a good case by God, before heaven.
But by God here with small gods and less heaven
my claim comes to this low court of spring grass.
Slow crocus, you have nothing to tell us,
snowdrop melt away in green peace, forgetfulness,
be still above my son. He's gone
early to bed and needs his rest like any man.
Little buds stop growing here or he'll make me go home,
and orphan my grief to wail at the sky door
of that angel who passed us for a lesser miracle,
a saint's ascent, the creation of some world.

PRO PATRIA MORI

Our city has never been bombed from the air—
long live our city! Sly providential fathers
always ship the war into enemy territory,
Tripoli, Nagasaki, The Balkans, Berlin,
their battlefields, their soldiers, their porcelain cities.
But we have our civic monuments to pain.

On my street a roofless mystery of brick
looks from a shot-through tower over the town.
Old brick, you climbed the air on the shoulders of giants
and will survive my bewilderment, holding your own
against the damnation of rain, adverse starlight
and curses of enemies weary from oceans of travel,
enemies long dead or aged to lean demons of rancor.
If ghosts had the power of death they were born with
there'd be more ruin here and less mystery.

I like to know my neighbors. So
I introduced myself in the wild yard
whose bushes have made a pace against invaders,
and waited to hear the ruin tell me its name
and origins, but got no comment. Just an ad
painted in slick billboard style of the twenties:
"Cloud Mattresses, the sleep that is forever,"
and a fading girl
dreaming in the sky against the wall.

Nobody knew it for anything but a ruin.
You'd think the builder had nothing more in mind
than a refuge for lost thoughts, or a rich joke
  on passers-by with nothing better to do
than ponder the reasons for unreasonable things.

    There is a guardian Saint of idlers
who loves me like a son. He must have sent the ghost
   who climbed my curiosity with me
into that penitentiary of galleried stillness.

His voice was as soft as my own thoughts:
"They are all gone, the women who manned the machines,
asleep in the sky or riding some senescent island
  of guiltlessness. When they were young
they made death for a living.

They left the world behind like a column of nuns
habited spare of trinkets and silken dainty
    underthings that might kiss a spark between their legs
and blow them all into heaven.
The roof was thin sheet metal, to that purpose,
the walls of their cubicles earth-worked iron-strong,
jaws of a monster cannon
  to shoot them up and out, so one girl's mistake
wouldn't blow the whole bomb factory like a bomb.

On this floor they worked in threes like the fates.
One girl fills a brass cup with the powder,
one weighs the charge and hands it on to a third
    who stitches the muffin bag for howitzer cannon.
Now, on to the second story—the powder rooms, the vats
from which death drifted in seas, dropped in dumbwaiters.
Black haze. A girl who wore her vanity for a cap
struck a match for her cigarette on the way home
and her dusty coiffure went off like a flashbulb.

The top story, that now opens on the sky,
is still guarded by a locked brass door.
High level security. Old men outnumbered the women
there, and the workers were larger than their machines.

How they must have believed in us, as they came to work
    in the mouth of this loaded cannon! Their precious work,
the words and ideas, the explaining
to generals, politicians, bombardiers,
to themselves and maybe to God, at that high level.

Who ever saw so many lightning rods
on a Christian building? One divine tantrum
might have blown us all into the arms of our enemies.
Now go home, my son. There's nothing more
to see or say, and your time is running out."

No, wait. What's above us? But now he's gone.
The sky is clear and blue through the air shaft,
through the stair windows, blue as the eyes of angels,
young angels, born young who died young and haunt good weather.

I don't believe the emptiness, my astonishment
keeps climbing the concrete stairs into lying silence,
sins of omission and abandonment,
looking for women working the death machines
or men thinking above them, men dying below.
Their nightmare pageantry is wasted on me.
I can't believe a word of it, a book,
a countryside of graves thrown from these ruins
or the dragon teeth of their broken, mythic stones.

YOUNG MEN'S GOLD

May, 1918. The speaker, a veteran of the Civil War, visits his wife's grave with his grandson, who is en route to join allied forces in France.

Time out of mind I have gone to light
  this flower from the bud-swirl of a new spring.
See how the old rose cracked from a year in the drawer?
Come along with me to St. Paul's, I know
the bush is blazing with them there, and then
there's so much to say before you go.
Think Julian, with your fresh strength
and an hour of an old man's past you'd be twice the man!

Is there a friend waiting for you?
Why all this rush?
                    To murder men
from such a distance you can't tell them from your friends.
Walk with me an hour. The train will wait
              or another train will take you on.

So much to say and who knows when we'll meet again
in such weather. A fine day to go to war!
And for me to make you this present of my past
that bites into my fist like this rose's spine.
Where old men relive their battles in dry words

around a cast iron stove that throws more heat,
I have kept my peace.
I could never cheat my solitude of its terrors
and I did my bragging at your age. Ah Julian,
this slaughter of men you've never seen
might shake you out of a youthful dream or two.
But killing a man you love with your hands, that
is no busy work of a dream but a live nightmare
that blasts a torture chamber in your soul.

Roland was my brother—not by blood—although
the Indian custom once dared us
draw blood from our wrists and join them under the moon.
He was the son of Charles Baldwin of Severn Cross Roads,
a merchant, rich in hard cash and a coastal fleet,
whose grandfather had sat in the Court of the Queen's Bench.
My father was a hunter and a smith. They shared
a river, a wall of rolled stones
and a faith in law that kept the boundary straight.

But Roland and I strove in all our games
as if our lawless wills had seized
premature inheritance, swelled and longed to burst
each into the frontier of the other's home.
I coveted his horse and he my guns;
I envied him his marksmanship and he

my skill in the breaking of horses and ease in the paces.
We ran our horses over the hills in the green summers
    flank to flank, their silken manes flowing in harmony
as if they had nodded agreement in the stalls
        to grant neither of us cause for pride.
He rode high-handed but he aimed with a dead eye.
We shattered a thousand green bottles into shards,
    breathing the rank gunpowder smoke shoulder to shoulder;
        his perfect eye making a match for my perfect pistols.
No one lost and we grew strong in the love of conflict
        and the hard passion a boy mistakes for a man's hatred.
When time came for us to quarrel in the way of men
        over a girl we forgot fast,
Roland rode off to Antietam with the Union.
My family, jammed at the border of the fight
        had plenty of blood to shed on either side
and tried to keep me home.

I spent my twenty-second winter clearing land
then set out restless along Chicone Creek in April.
Coming from Swann Gut I made my way
      through ironwood forests and sought Okihanikan Cove
near Bloodsworth Isle, where the manifold race
            whips back on itself in sunlight.
I hauled water there for nuns in meditation, nuns
kneeling black and white in the dim light
  of a room wainscotted with human bones.
Four thigh bones forming a diamond inlaid the clay wall

and five human skulls set within. As if
one's thin-clad skeleton were shy latticework
for the climbing soul, and one's own ribs
too frail a cage for taming the furious heart.
I served there and ate their gruel for seven weeks
then poled a raft to Pokata Creek
where the water runs clear and open
to Mattawoman Creek shallows and land where the going is bad.
I followed steep-banked Acquango, the Ending River
to Quantico where Indians dance on the long inlet.

Came over a squat knoll near the town
and stopped at a low clearing.
There stood three slack-jawed yokels kicking at a corpse
sprawled old and naked in the mud—
more like the clay
he'd come to than the man he'd been.
I asked how this dung-pile had offended them
and got more questions for answers:
who in hell was I, what was the dead man to me?

Well this is no way to treat a man, dead or alive.
I drew a cocked pistol, sighted down
the barrel a fat belly
and asked them softer this time.

One grinned and said the corpse had owed him rent.
        One grunted that the man had owed a horse.
                The third held markers on a gambling debt.

"Gambler," I said, "the wheel spin or turn of a card
that finds you breathing, your rival dead, is no losing game.
Landlord, what a greasy tool of a host,
            mislaying the tenant's baggage, suppose
he sends for it later, orders
     a sight-draft on hell's coffers to square his debt—
will you journey into such weather to get it cashed?
And you horse-trader, or as like a foul horse-thief
          (no man who defies a corpse's deed to the earth
                  would honor a cash receipt)
did this horse so love the rider
          that its spirit outlept horseflesh, bit and saddle
to catch him as he fell out of the world?
Then your horse rides at stronger hands than yours,
rest easy."

Then I emptied my pockets of gold all on the ground,
tossed the coins in the pattern of a man
and bid these ghouls dig deep with their nails
under the gold. Till the grave was man-sized and deep,
the skin of their hands all broken and bleeding.
Then they laid the corpse in the earth and filled him in.

Two days later I crossed Cherry Run and climbed North Mountain.
Slept there in the crags my first night free of dreams.
And on the road at daybreak fell in
with a limping grey wall-eyed gun peddler
whose white mule rattled with a load of hardware.
He takes a shine to me. "Are you on the way
to war, or to court that girl in Shepherdstown?"
he says, and slaps his mule. "One battle's as good
as the next, as the corporal says, and I've met men
were going either way, but not a man returning.
All my guns, and not a man worth killing.
They do not love the dead as they did
or the killing, or loving.
Men are no more what they were, my boy, no more,
but the guns are better.

"Have you been to Shepherdstown?
There's a little lady there in heat, has set
every pup down wind of her baying at the moon
and at the darkness when the moon is gone.
I passed by there to sell her father guns.
I saw her through the crowd of men, and thanked my years
I've paid most of my life and bought me free
of one sure rein of madness.
There's a dragon in her body
no young man could see

beneath those breasts that ride so high above her stays,
a breech that fills her corset near to bursting, not
          from excess, but sheer love of it.
A fatal archery in her lips,
               the blue-palmed petals of her eyelids,
light fingered flowers of her eyes.

     She pricks your fancy? She's a piece
for Gods and senators to breed on,
               boys and old men to dream on
and a fair match for a man with the heart to play her right.
          Oh men are no more what they were, my boy
               no more! She says she'll have
     no husband but a man
who's gotten through this war alive.
And so she'll take a fancy to some buck
and have his ring and peck him on the cheek
          and pack him off to Manassas or Fredericksburg.
Thus she is six times widowed who was never wed.
Her beauty is a double threat luring brave souls
     with odds against their living to hold the prize.
          All my guns, and not a man worth killing!
               Who loves the dead as he should,
                    or the killing, or loving?
The guns are better."

He tethered his mule to a tree
and laid his guns out on the grass:
smooth bone-handled Colt revolvers that balance themselves
in your hand, Carbines from Carolina
stamped on the lockplate with branching palmettos,
muzzle-loading rifle muskets with gunstocks
of claret-grained walnut
the steel trigger
bent like a rearing horse or a perched bird.
I had my eye on a Leech and Rigdon
rifled seven grooves left,
of steel inlaid with gold and a fire-blued barrel.
But I'd thrown my last coin into the stranger's grave.

"Now lad a gun's a gun. I've sold an arsenal
to men who'll never live to pay me off."
He reached into his saddlebag and pulled
out a sword that battled beam for beam with the sun.
The pommel and grip were bright gold cast as a lady
whose shining hair and robes flow to the cross-guards.
The knuckle bows were openwork silver
coiling serpents that strike at her skirts.
She crosses her thigh with a gold sword in her grip
and pricks it into the snake head by her left foot.
Two pinpoint blue-black sapphires shine for her eyes.

"No man could pay for this. And now it's yours.
Blacken the hilt with paint to hide the gold.
You're not on the way to a ball.
And what's gold
shines in your hand when there's a debt to pay,
whether it moves in the darkness or the light.
That sword is better than the best of guns
that are better today by far than the best of men.
Now promise me if this should save your life
you'll remember me on your wedding night.
When that girl lies bare beside you in the sheets,
each point and turn of her smooth flesh candlelit,
save a life's portion of the live girl
for an old man who'd shrivel and waste
if ever once he thought he'd had his last."

Nothing mattered then so much to me
as this vow of grace to the old man.
So I promised him, belted the sword and rode away.

I moved on to Shepherdstown and a white manor
where carriages stood at the gate and horses grazed
waiting for the tournament of men
ram-rod straight in grey shell jackets,
caged and pacing back of veranda columns.

And a fine-boned woman gazed beyond them
          from their midst, a beauty
fed on wisdom that her age defied.
No sorrow had left its mark on her face
               nor laughter, though she freely laughed.
Passions that line and cross the cheeks and brow
      lived in youthful harmony there
as if every wrinkle knew its complement,
        and gave way before it leaving the girl unmarred.
Full moon radiant
for a carousel of shooting stars, she shone
with a cold light that kindled and froze them fast.

I stayed until the last of them had gone, and she
   looked where stars were rising between the hills.
She spoke as if the dying day were her councilor
and turned to me only as the night came on.

"Day after day they return, crowding this house,
throng the veranda like a herd of mooning deer.
each one waiting for a word.
As if my voice were magic and my thought
had eyes to read the last sentence of their dreams.

"I have waited for this silence all day long
and now break it into pieces of words for a total stranger.
I cannot turn away a guest
who comes in love and good faith,
but I haven't the heart to name one and condemn him.

They think they love me and want to die for this:
the darkness of love is more terrible than death.
Suppose one moves me and I say as much
and recite my father's law that our desire
be tempered in gunfire. Suppose he dies
as six of my suitors have died before him?
Then my speech has killed
all that he wished for and his half of the wishes too.
Old women mutter curses in the street
that catch in my head and rattle the whole way home.
Grandmothers, maiden aunts and bygone sweethearts
of men they say have gone to war for me.

The first was a boy I loved before the war,
shy one, with his eyes half-closed as if sifting light
on what little past or future his soul could reach.
The son of a rich man,
he asked for me, my father gave me freely
though neither of us was old enough
to know love beyond head-on glances that fast fell.

War came on and broke up the marriage plan,
cheapened my dowry—
were the young soldier killed I could be left
his father's charge, better to wait,
let the boy return and stand by his own vow.
Typhoid carried him off before the fighting
and I was left to mourn, oh

so briefly; what little there is of a woman
in a girl's love, a shot seed that ricochets,
pierces a new heart and strikes root there!

The second was an older boy hot on the road to manhood
who wanted my love
as a silent axle to his journey's rolling wheel.
He knew me for a month and conquered me
with a trick of his kisses to linger on my flesh
and satisfy me to wait for the next though he leave
me waiting till my lips and hair frost over.
The third was his brother, an older lover still
as my love grew old;
he came to tell me of his brother's death
and held me while I sobbed into his coat.

When the third was killed I crushed the telegram
and bolted up the high stairs to the attic.
I looked out furious on the land
and watched the sun fall lost in the blue hills
and screamed, and would not come down.
When I did I hated them and my venomous passion,
dreamed of my lovers and their fathers and my own
all naked in a cage,
tearing each other's flesh with knives and eating it
until there was only one
who looking like none of them was the size of all,
who laughed like the moon and with each breath
grew smaller then, until the cage was bare.

My next three lovers were proper men
        as I was a lady then
with manners to protect me from my heart.
I was free to say I loved them
    whether I did or not.

So the new suitor clicks his heels on the parquet
and swears he'll swallow his weight in bullets
and carry me off to the bridal suite.
As if my love or his were strong enough
to turn aside cannonfire.
If this were true what would the battle prove?
If love could keep one man alive

no man would set his sights on another's life. My own
has shown me six times over that love dies too."

"Lady I have no more to offer you
    than a vow composed of wishes and prophecy.
We'll call our vow a spell
to free you of these walking ghosts
        who lie to you and promise you their lives,
and the flying ghosts that come to you grey from battle.
I'm leaving without a care for living; should I return
you will know I'm another man, one
        you may take for a husband or refuse.
Count my words the ill-spoken sorrow that knows yours,
my love a remembrance of your voice
and eyes from a life some dream has run across
        as a lighthouse beam sets worlds of the sea aglow."

Bore tide, sea pulse in blind scraps,
sea-sturgeon, bluefish spin in green domes of colliding tides.
Not only women move to the moon's song
but young men as well, who have come to the end of a thought.
This is the time a young man looks for death,
when the roads have all gone by him and the women
    overlap like sea waves colored on the beach
after the surge has struggled to drag him under.
He has ridden the women like high waves on the surf,
        leaving them when they break

to paint a story in brine and frail shells on the sand.
This is the age a young man looks for death
        knowing no more of the game
than a boy set adrift in a cockleboat angling for fish
        with a hickory branch and tangled twine.
He has watched through dawn mist from the shore
and never seen the pale bait flash between the waves.
It is not old men who send young men to war
    but an obscene battle chorus of young and old
railing at life through a single throat.
The tongue that dips so sweetly in life's mouth
shrinks back when he learns she's death's whore.
It is not that old men send young men to war
    in hatred, but old men so love what they were—
and this is the age a young man hunts death, prizing
his own above all others, dreams of it, sings
in nightmares carved more perfectly in their pain
                than any living war.
While he lifts his murder cry above battle-racket,
a secret death wish swells his shirt with pride
like a packet of scented promises of love
that can't be kept, won't stop a bullet.

I joined the rebel army near Charlestown. In good time
they made me a captain, supplied my company
with Mississippi and Deringer rifles
and sent us to break up a band of federals lodged in a gorge

of Blue Ridge, not a mile from Swift Run Gap.
Skirmished three days there without doing them damage
for they took to the sides of the mountain
where the ground fell too rugged.
Jackson sent Captain Jones in command
of three platoons of sharpshooters and two field pieces
and he drove them into Green County across the mountains.
Late September, the golden-wheeled daisies crowded the roadsides.
And I took my troop into Page Valley to scout
Luray and Front Royal. At daybreak
with long clouds sweeping to the sky's margin
we reached the western post,
unsaddled our horses, led them to swim the Shenandoah
and poled men and saddles across in a rotted gondola.
Then marched to the edge of Clark County
and laid by all day.

Stars brightening above us, we headed for Millwood
where the enemy camp lay sprawled under cover of night.
But at sunrise crossing the bridge we were nearly surrounded;
cavalry had come down from White Post
cutting us off. Escaped by a mountain path under leaning cliffs,
each man looking for death in ambuscade from the rock-tops.
Climbed the Blue Ridge into Rappahanock County
and thence to Swift Run Gap.

A mile and a half from the Springs I heard hoof-beats
of a courier who cried as he rode "go back, go back!"

    and a great cloud of dust rolled up through a gap in the trees.
No sooner wheeled our horses than the enemy
        broke forth from the woods a quarter mile from our rear.
I called to my men to hurry across the bridges
while Welch and I held them back with shots from our pistols.
Then we followed on down the reserve and found Fletcher's company
and as I passed
he asked me to ride down with him in the charge.

The forces met like granite trains colliding,
the earth shuddered horses rolled,
their teeth bared, nostrils wide, their wailing drowned out
by profane cries of the men and thunder of gunfire.
These were men I knew in my youth and I see them
as if they were going down before my eyes.
Michael Keegan killed Valentine Williard with a quick bullet,
Valentine, born in St. Mary's the son of a jurist,
                        who had dreamed through his youth of a battle.
But Keegan blasted him right off through the smooth skin
of his cheek and the minie-ball shattered the Pallatine bone
and knocked his blond head back like a Sunday punch
and Valentine never knew what hit him.
And Benedict Johnson shot Jesse Roach in the hip
where the saber dangled in the brass scabard, but Roach
never saw the blade bare, for the bullet passed clean through
the groin tendons so he doubled up like a slug,
blood spurted and he fell groaning from the saddle.

And Johnson killed John Kelly with his second shot,
then killed Amos Wallman of Howard County, the son
of Richard and kind Margaret Gassaway
who had wept a full week when Amos left for Antietam
and couldn't be comforted, with wine, or the bible.
Johnson blew a fifty-eight caliber shell through his shoulder
and a hole a surgeon could fit four fingers in.
And the bullet drove through, and the blood and cartilage with it,
spattering the lathered thigh of his rearing stallion.
War wrung the sweet life out of this man
and his soul was sucked into the heavens.
William Tingstrom saw Amos roll from the rearing stallion.
His heart went out then flared like a wind-blown coal,
for he had known Amos in his boyhood when they
tilled the patchwork fields of the Ellicott City farms,
hauling grain and corn to the Baltimore market.

And Tingstrom swore and emptied his hand gun
at Johnson's dark head, three shots missed
but one cracked the parietal bone and took the scalp
and one shell burned through Johnson's eye
that had looked down the spine of his pistol selecting its victims.
So Johnson reeled from the saddle and hit the ground
and was beaten into dust under horses' hooves.
So the armies rushed together and whirled in a clamor
as a sea invades a river at bore tide
and speeds at the shallowing channel
yet will not be turned under,

and the steepening wave front collapses in a welter of foam
and continues to rush up river.

And I hung fire and watched through the dust clouds and gunsmoke,
could have sworn I saw Roland's head, and waited
to blow it clean from his shoulders.

My company struck at log-pens and rifle pits.
We charged through two grain fields across a lane
        and crowded the base of a hill.
When we started I rode well to the rear of the column
but no horse alive could match the speed of my sorrel
and I was the first to leap into the redoubt,
firing point blank into the gunner's face.

Then we fell in line under sharp fire from Bolivar.
Ashby had gained the heights on the center and right
and ordered me to command a captured gun.
I ran the ponderous gun under Bolivar's nose
        and gave them grape and cannister in turn.
Troops rode out to back them, artillery sounding
            the cannonade, thunderclap on hollow boom.

Two minie-balls crashed through our limber-box,
          one struck the harness breeching of a wheel horse.

I loaded a solid shot and cut the fuse
            to explode when the enemy rode to charge my cannon
and stood ready to fire when I saw
                the linstock had sputtered out. I swore
I'd have another shot and ran to the gunner's fire,
picked up a live coal in my fingers
   and stuck it in the touch hole.
The shell flew crashing through a column
                  jammed full of the enemy and killed eleven.
Then they opened on us with two field pieces, scattering
              our force of supporting dragoons.
I spiked the twenty-four pounder and left it there
            for all the good it could do them.

Riding out I saw Roland's head rise out of the ranks.
His mare rose on her hindquarters as he yanked the reins,
wailing as the cruel bit drew blood from her jaws.
A bow-shaped saber gleamed in his right hand
for the fighting had emptied his pistol.
We charged, met eye to eye over the horses' heads, his sword
crashed down on mine that rose aslant to meet him.
Steel slid on steel to the hilts, gold striking brass,
      and we stood frozen in our power,
blades locked crosswise, pressing wrist on wrist,
broke free and the steel crashed again above our heads, once,
    twice and I lunged for the prize that was his heart.

His saber fell, he leaned into the wound, my sword
drenched to the gold hilt in his blood.
I felt our love and hatred for the last time
shudder up the length of the steel blade,
and a youth dead at either end.

There were other battles but my memory has made them
so many dances of death in a hollow mountain under the sea.
As if another man had fought them
or the spirit of some man I'd killed
had ghost written and posted them through the mail.
So once in a while a nightmare surfaces
like black shrapnel from a cauterized wound.

Shall I say I cried, what was the truth of my sorrow?
My separate victory stood out of my army's ranks
like the shell-shocked soldier who rises out of a dugout
and raises his fist to the skies and curses God.
Shall I say I rejoiced, with the cause
for happiness dead at the end of my hand,
a man I had to kill to know I loved,
my brothers dead, defeated on every side?
The fight had gone out of me, there was nothing
left for my heart to beat against.

I rode to Shepherdstown in the spring
to see her in the daylight,

the lady who'd come to walk with me between nightmares.
She had outgrown her mourning clothes.
Though a child might sweat as much as the father
for the father's cause,
when he loses she cannot cry so many tears.

There was life in her I had not known
and a life in me she knew I had forgotten.
There was a clear stream rounded her home to the west.
We would stroll there and wade in the cold current
and through blue-eyed grasses that made a bed
for goat's rue and blue jasmine
and lovers who might tumble there
reaching to gather the blossoms for a bouquet.
She was all my longing had made of her, but wonderfully strange
as the dream a sleeper weaves
from the circus of lights between his mind and the darkness
the way ancient shepherds figured stars into a myth
to draw heaven close and warm their sleepless nights.

The night we were wed I dreamed I saw
the lit face of the gunpeddler at our bedfoot.
I reached for my sword. He spoke: "Not so fast—
I am the man who gave you that sword
when you hadn't a red cent to buy my guns.
And Roland might have had the best of you there
with a pistol. The sword gave your hand weight.

I willed it to you out of gratitude
for I am the man you buried with your gold.
And we dead are as the flowers that rely
on the good will of the earth to see them
up through the stem again
alive on the air!
I've come for the soft prize you promised me,
your wife, the fair part of her treasures you can share."

My impulse was to swing at him with the sword
but second thoughts
made me lie still awhile and dream an answer.
If this were the spirit of the buried man
let him have that part of the woman a spirit can hold.
No living man can be jealous of the dead.

"Old man I thank you for my life and bride.
But did you give her out of gratitude
only to take her from me now she's mine?
For all that I know of women I couldn't choose
what part of her is most precious to me now.
How might I divide her least painfully
and pay my debt?

If her soul and body be of equal worth
between this world and the next—

then take the body sleeping at my side
                with all the night wrapped around her,
the world in her arms,
for it is beyond me how I can part with her spirit."

Then the red smile vanished and the face
and I awoke, or first I woke and saw no face
but the woman breathing evenly beside me
and moonlight on the marriage lace and silk.

Winter passed. She grew more beautiful with each season.
I would have sworn I had outwitted the dead man.
April rained by, the head-on light of May
        raised violets. The love words
only stopped at our lips in the night where our souls
            were bound somewhere between us.
She grew round with my child in her, and I was full
as the roiling concourse of two swollen rivers
            when springfloods sluice away the mountain snow.
In the white room where we first came together,
        she came to term, delivering
her own death, and your father living, into my arms.

I have held you long enough. Is there a friend
        waiting for you? Could be that quiet girl
you keep a secret from everyone but me, perhaps
she can whisper what I cannot speak.

Whom did I choose to murder,
whom have I loved?
What can I give you who would bring me grief?
Ground shards from the wreckage of my youth, a fist of sand
a child brings home to remind us of the sea,
dry grains that slip the mind of an hourglass.
I have found at the point of the thorn
all that the rose denied.
I light this bud from the last; have I taken
her spirit in my heart these fifty years?
I have been through the fires of hell
and brought back only one candle.

1974

OLD MAN AT THE WOOD'S EDGE

Leaves, dry skirt of the wind, lie down by me
        and don't blow away.
Sky is low, the sun's in hiding,
        this masterless winter like a cataract
of broken days, has made
                a tombstone quarry of these hills.
The woods are full of skeletons and the closets
are full of orphaned saplings, birds
nursed in their chilled arms, perched
        on their white shoulders.

I made this cold in the raw image of my absence
so that I might know revenge for my own death.
It is a violent, senseless act, like all acts of love.
I hang the moon in my heart,
                sweep the sky of stars.
My children must learn to find their way in the dark.
I am a hard river, a misfortune
                        without pity. When I go down
I'm taking the summer with me.

OLD MAN BY THE RIVER

Flood tide, boats glide high above the bank,
 gay lilies crane to look into the sun.
What kind of friends would leave me here alone,
an empty house behind me, a full graveyard
ranging from my door to the garrulous river?
Kind friends, and true, to leave me with my thoughts.
My teeth are gone, my hair's a white cyclone;
I have more secrets than heaven will ever know.
Take my daffodils, what a bargain of light
for the reckless April that discovers them!
Little girls with lightning-quick hands
arrest the leaping blossoms in mid-flight
and lay them on my doorstep in the night.
Today I scared the boy who brings the news.
I am a weathered man the adventure of whose
 conversation nature has immured.
Three walls are deadpan stone, the last is the river.
Who will I talk to when the river runs away?

RIP VAN WINKLE

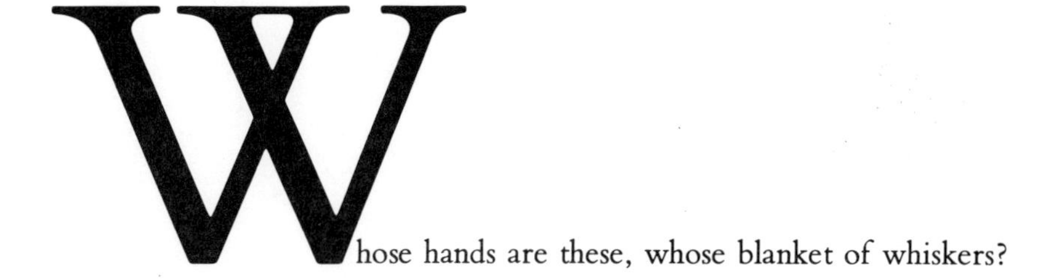
hose hands are these, whose blanket of whiskers?

I must have fallen a long way in my sleep
to land in this circle of wild phlox.
Last I remember it was autumn
and I was in a young man's rage
over some woman, I have forgotten,
who sent a floating puppet of herself
to tell me she would never come again.
When she had gone I lay down in this grove
and sleep came over me like a gentling music.

Now I've slept the heart of my life away
and nothing to show for it but this dream:
I swore I'd take these faithless woods alive
to burn like a candle in the attic
of my remorse. And all I vowed was by my will
as good as done. I climbed the fire tower
and saw it all go to hell,
leaf by leaf, mountain by mountain, storm by storm,
every elm bark and wind that knew her name.

It's better for the birds I slept so long.
Sure as hell I would have burned this forest down
and lived to be more lonely than I am.

Better to wake on the right side of one's life
in a clear season, and see the forest for the trees,
    each one in complete possession of itself.
The years I lost are winter to this spring.
It's good green, and a kind shade for my old head.

ECHO

The wind that leaves the fisherman in peace
assaults the blue hills, the wooded mountain
like a caravan of gypsies in old Fords
abandoning Illinois
to plunder the rural groceries of New England.

So the man at sea-level can look the sea in the eye
and know his own power, vis-a-vis
tame breakers making their mark against his shore.
Whereas the high numbers of the upland storm
howl through the breathless zero of one's will.

Right now a tree is falling and nobody to catch it
but a sleeping tramp, a maverick gypsy cipher
who's forgotten who and where he is,
his mother and child, the birdsong and mayapple,
the sun on his cheeks and the path he took to bed.

SUMMER HOUSE

1

Miles from town the long arm of the world
pursues me in the disguise of rivers and meadows,
a cheap trick she plays but I have to laugh
        and go along for the ride.
Same light and wind and wind and light,
            heroes who make the history of the day.
Clouds exiled from Northern storms
                glide out from the nape of a mountain,
white targets on a shooting gallery range.
Ladders of getaway light drop from the clouds.

2

Old eagle mounts cross-drafts over the pines
        circling for slow rabbits,
young hawk scouts a ravine for challenges.
Sheep strum a field of waking daisies,
    pluck spikelets of couch grass;
day lilies chafe high collars of dagger fronds.
Mad architect pitched my roof at the world's end
and like Noah I want to bring everything into the house,
        at least a photo and a name for each,
light for my walls and a spell against silence.

3

But something resists, Great Nature or my little one
like a rich man's mistress embarrassed suddenly
by her position in the scheme of his affections.
When power drives the body to acts of love,
        love takes the first flight out.
And the best company, like the worst, arrives uninvited.
There is the heart's desire for a full house and then
there is the danger of friends as the leaves of the forest
veiling the dance of naked trees,
the skeleton with whom you must at last lie down.

4

When mind is coterminal with nature's body
they hum like spent lovers in a bed of silence, rich
        as suspended applause, or counsel
so wise and potent we reserve it for ourselves.
Such full loneliness presages cordial death.
But this house reminds me I am far from home.
Men in strict training for a meaner death
keep to themselves like this
in solemn imitation of their enemy, hoping
he'll think they're part of him and pass on.

5

I would be a better neighbor to the unknown
if I could round up the vagabonds of my world
and take them on the road with me when I go
to some ghost town that has forgotten
the jugglers of the wind, the high-handed clown
of sunshine, the stallion of love that leaps the hoop
flaming eternally between my life and death.
Surely we're allowed to take what we can carry
and maybe my show would bring children to the streets
and women to the windows of that sleeping town.

6

Night has slipped under the blanket of the lake.
Tideless waves throw wings of light on the sandy floor,
    nerve on nerve of gold underwater birds.
Earth's historians, wind and light protect their sources.
But I'll bet wind comes from the spaces dead men leave
        and raw light rises from tombs.
Too gothic perhaps, but I swear
there is no greater truth in the storm and sun
whose riddles surround us like the horizon
no man can see without turning his back on it.

SUNDAY

When the bat got in before dawn
he brought the darkest of the night with him.
Wings beat whispers above our bed
        and a vigilant instinct woke us shuddering.
Radar told us something was flying around
up there and it was no nightmare
but the very form of fear, its content unknown,
a shadow strayed from the cave and the church tower.
I opened the window but he stayed with us
      circling the room like a black halo
until daybreak when he could glide out on the wings
        of our vision, a brighter way of flying.